MARC MAJEWSKI

Butterfly
Child

KATHERINE TEGEN BOOKS
An imprint of HarperCollins Publishers

I am a butterfly!

One final touch . . .

. . . and I am
ready to go.

I let the wind carry me
from flower to flower.

When I open my wings . . .

. . . I spin and swirl

and twist and twirl

and flutter and flap.

DOINK!

Oh no . . .

. . . not these kids again.

"Leave me alone!"

Fine!

I'd rather stay
home anyway.

By myself.

Knock,
knock!

"Here . . . ," Papa says.

"Now . . ."

". . . what are we going to do?"

"Start over," I say.

We pick and patch

and stitch and sew

and drip and draw.

Papa smiles.
"You are a butterfly child!"

One final touch . . .

. . . and I am ready to go.

I let the wind carry me.

And this time . . .

. . . when I open my wings . . .

. . . I fly!